W9-CHS-652

This book belongs to

_____

The Easter Bunny

RETOLD BY

Louise Betts Egan

ILLUSTRATED BY

Debbie Dieneman

ARIEL BOOKS

ANDREWS AND McMEEL

KANSAS CITY

Library of Congress Cataloging-in-Publication Data

Betts, Louise.
    The Easter Bunny / retold by Louise Betts Egan ; illustrated by
Debbie Dieneman.
        p.   cm.
    "Ariel books."
    Summary: Three little rabbits roam through the forest searching for
the mysterious Easter Bunny, who continues to elude them.
    ISBN 0-8362-4935-6 : $6.95
    [1. Rabbits—Fiction. 2. Easter—Fiction. 3. Stories in rhyme.]
I. Dieneman, Debbie, ill. II. Title.
PZ8.3.B4644Eas   1993
[E]—dc20   92-32435
                                                                    CIP
                                                                     AC

Design: Susan Hood and Mike Hortens
Art Direction: Armand Eisen, Mike Hortens, and Julie Phillips
Art Production: Lynn Wine
Production: Julie Miller and Lisa Shadid

The Easter Bunny

This is a tale about a tail—
Which may sound rather funny—
But here is how three rabbits set out
To find the Easter Bunny.

The little rabbits were munching on grass
Around a tall oak tree;
Daisy, Dandy, and Fluff were friends,
But they simply could not agree.

"The Easter Bunny lives in a tree trunk!"
"No, a burrow—lined all in gold!"
"And he wears a silk vest (only the best)—"
"That's not what I was told!"

Their chatting and squabbling grew quite loud
Until all of the forest cried, "Stop!"
"But I've always wondered," admitted the deer,
"Does he fly? Or does he hop?"

Such questions baffled the creatures
And set the forest astir.
"Whoooo has seen him?" inquired the owl.
No one could say for sure.

Now, the day was cold and dreary,
Though buds were on the trees;
Snow had long since melted
Yet winter chilled the breeze.

Just thinking of the Easter Bunny
Made them dream of spring—
Of fuzzy chicks and soft, warm grass
And the pretty eggs he'd bring.

"We've got to find him!" Daisy said,
Hippity-hopping 'round the tree;
"Hey, I'll join you!" Dandy called,
As Fluff cried, "Wait for me!"

Through the forest sped the word,
By song and growl and coo,
That three young rabbits were on the hunt
For the mysterious you-know-who.

14

For days they wandered through the woods,
They searched near and far beyond:
They followed paths and forged ahead
Until they spied a pond.

They scampered toward the water—
Hopping a mossy log.
When suddenly before them
Appeared a giant frog.

He said, "To catch the Easter Bunny,
As he hops along his trail,
Take this magic shaker of salt
And shake some on his tail."

The rabbits were very weary,
But with the shaker in Fluff's hand,
They felt certain any minute
They'd find Easter Bunny Land.

But what do you think happened
To our trusty rabbits three?
They sank down on some soft green grass
And fell asleep beneath a tree!

And in the warm and dewy morn'
When they opened up their eyes,
Dandy, Fluff, and Daisy
Were in for a surprise.

Spring had sprung upon the forest,
All leaves and daffodils;
Blue sky peeked through the branches,
Birds warbled their new trills.

And before the 'wakening threesome
Sat three baskets all a-brim
With colored eggs and candies,
And bedecked in golden trim.

Now, listen closely, children—
This isn't quite the end,
Beside the baskets lay a note
Signed, "From your long-eared friend."

"Oh, you may search for magic,"
Said the note, "over hill and vale,
But catching it is just as hard
As shaking salt upon my tail."